The Only
Alex Addleston
in All These Mountains

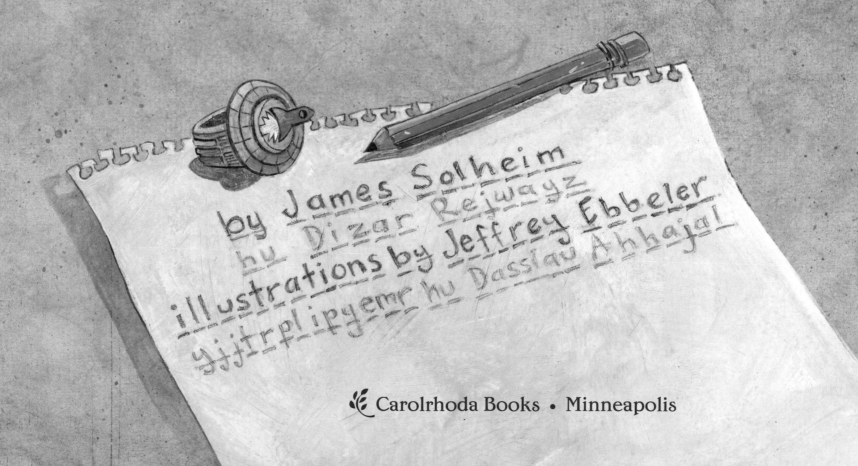

by James Solheim

hu Dizar Rejwayz

illustrations by Jeffrey Ebbeler

yjjtrplipyemr hu Dasslau Ahhajal

Carolrhoda Books • Minneapolis

Carolrhoda Books
A division of Lerner Publishing Group, Inc.
241 First Avenue North
Minneapolis, MN 55401 U.S.A.

For reading levels and more information, look up this title at www.lernerbooks.com.

Main body text set in Adrianna 17/24.
Typeface provided by Chank.

Library of Congress Cataloging-in-Publication Data

Solheim, James.
    The only Alex Addleston in all these mountains / by James Solheim ; illustrations
by Jeffrey Ebbeler.
        p.   cm.
    Summary: From the moment they meet in their Flatt Mountain kindergarten
classroom, Alex and Alex are best friends, and even though they are later separated
for six years, their friendship remains unbroken.
    ISBN 978–1–4677–0346–8 (lib. bdg. : alk. paper)
    ISBN 978–1–4677–2400–5 (eBook)
    [1. Best friends—Fiction. 2. Friendship—Fiction.] I. Ebbeler, Jeffrey, illustrator.
II. Title.
PZ7.S689Onl 2014
[E]—dc23   2013019976

Manufactured in the United States of America
1 – DP – 12/31/13

For Justin, Jenny, and Joyce—with thanks to Anna Cavallo,
Andrew Karre, Zach Marell, and Jeffrey Ebbeler for their insights
that brought the book to life —J.S.

For Dave, my biggest fan —J.E.

Alone among twenty children, Alex Addleston searched the crowd for her desk. Today Alex was a kindergartner, on her own in a new school.

Then she saw it, shiny and inviting, with two words taped to the front: "Alex Addleston." *Her* desk.

Except a boy was sitting there. A boy with a name tag.

Alex looked at Alex's name tag. And Alex looked back. Alex Addleston and Alex Addleston were pretty sure they weren't each other. Yet their name tags said they were.

Laughing, Alex and Alex squirmed into the same seat. The teacher brought in another desk, but Alex wouldn't switch. Neither would Alex.

The teacher's eyes smiled. "You can share, just for today."

That afternoon, for the first time ever, two Alex Addlestons bounced up Bug Tussle Road to fill bucket after bucket with blueberries.

That evening, for the first time ever, two Alex Addlestons chased Flatt Mountain fireflies till their jars glowed and lit their grins like the moon.

Alex and Alex did everything together.

They giggled in gym class and passed notes in the lunch line. They elected each other president and vice dinosaur. They collected frogs, turtles, and a big old crawdad couple named Mr. and Mrs. Sassafras Jorgensen.

Seal of the Dino President

"Let's always stay together," Alex told Alex as they swung on their swing in the old oak tree.

"And stay best friends."

"Okay, best friends."

They traded Captain Moonbeam message rings, coding a secret in each: "Harp slyamor, me zippal fwip." Which meant "Best friends, no matter what."

When June came, Alex's mom took him to Chicago to share the summer with his grandma. They would only be gone two months, but still . . . .

In Chicago, Alex drew pictures for Alex in his grandma's lap,

while Alex dreamed of Alex on the swing in the old oak tree.

Alex collected rocks near a lake as big as a sea,

while Alex gathered pet snails on a mossy rock above a creek.

Then the day came for Alex to return to Flatt Mountain. He clutched a gift he'd made for his friend. The car drove all night as he slept.

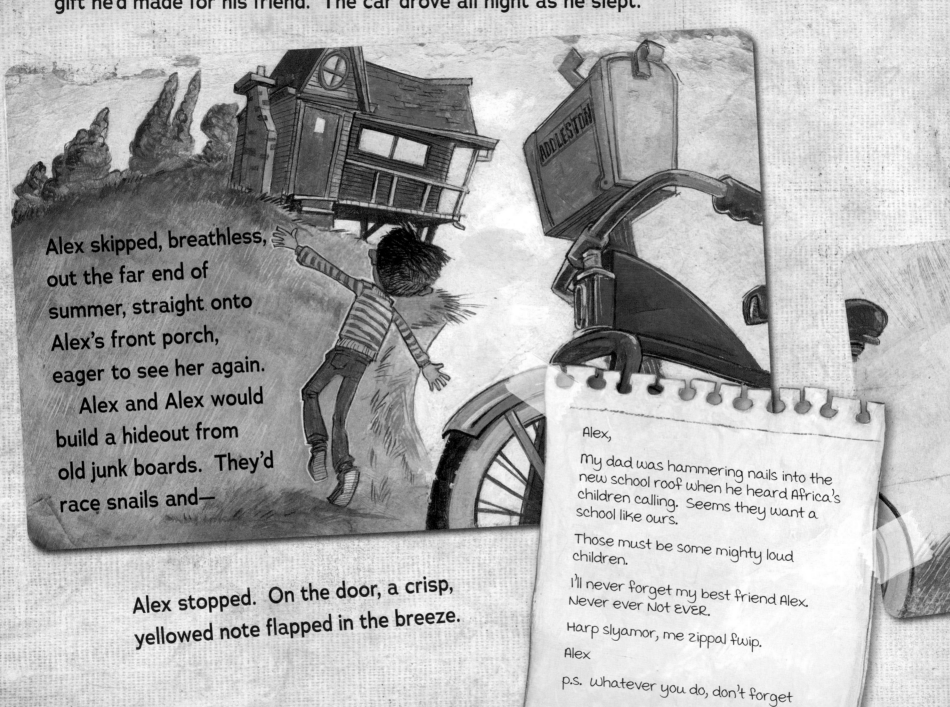

Alex skipped, breathless, out the far end of summer, straight onto Alex's front porch, eager to see her again.
Alex and Alex would build a hideout from old junk boards. They'd race snails and—

Alex stopped. On the door, a crisp, yellowed note flapped in the breeze.

Alex,

My dad was hammering nails into the new school roof when he heard Africa's children calling. Seems they want a school like ours.

Those must be some mighty loud children.

I'll never forget my best friend Alex. Never ever NOT EVER.

Harp slyamor, me zippal fwip.

Alex

p.s. Whatever you do, don't forget

Alex ran down the hill and up the mountain, looking for the rest of the note.

"Don't forget" couldn't be the end!

He chased the wind to the end of day, but he found nothing.

to write to me. My mom says to send letters to

Box 95086,
Kisii 058, Kenya,
until we get our house.

Alex lay in the grass on the mountaintop
and counted the stars—alone.

Alex lay in the grass on the savanna and counted the stars—alone.

Alex
(Flatt mountain)

Alex
(Kenya)

But Alex wasn't about to give Alex up just because a few zillion miles had come between them.

He still whispered to Alex as he wandered each day along the creek. He still cartwheeled through the cold grass, teaching her his favorite tricks. She never said no to a climb up a trembly birch tree.

They were Best Friends, No Matter What.

He made back-to-school presents for Alex, and May baskets for Alex, and birthday presents for Alex, and more back-to-school presents for Alex. A Popsicle-stick plane. A whistle whittled from a willow twig. Slowly, the pile on his dresser grew.

But Flatt Mountain's children called, with baseballs to throw and candles to blow— eight, nine, then ten on a chocolate cake.

Soon Alex only joined him when he was alone watching the dust dance in his bedroom window's slanted light, or when he walked to a magic place where vines slowly wound around a tattered tree swing.

Alex's finger grew too big for his Captain Moonbeam message ring. Into his pocket it went.

In Kenya, Alex wasn't about to give Alex up just because a few zillion miles had come between them.

She still whispered to Alex as she strolled each day along the creek. She raced through the village in games of hide-and-seek, always such a good hider that he never found her unless she giggled. He never said no to a climb up a Jackalberry tree.

One day, as she danced among the elephants, a fever joined the dance.

Alex walked into Alex's dreams, sneaking lemonade to her hospital bed and dancing her out into the cool rain. "Harp slyamor, me zippal fwip," Alex said and showed her his ring.

The fever stomped away, seeing it could never own her.

Alex woke with a smile.
"Alex's lemonade kept me
cool," she told the nurse.

The girl that Alex once knew spoke Swahili now. She loved to carve soapstone elephants and ride real elephants. She learned to make a soccer ball dance like the memory of a boy her mind could never quite touch.

The boy that Alex once knew sat close to his grandma each night. He told her old jokes to help her remember. He learned to make a fiddle bow flash like the dream of a girl his mind could never quite touch.

Alex's family moved to a new valley in Kenya. Alex's family moved three mountains over from Flatt Mountain. Alex and Alex were lost to each other.

Alex grew tall.

Alex grew tall.

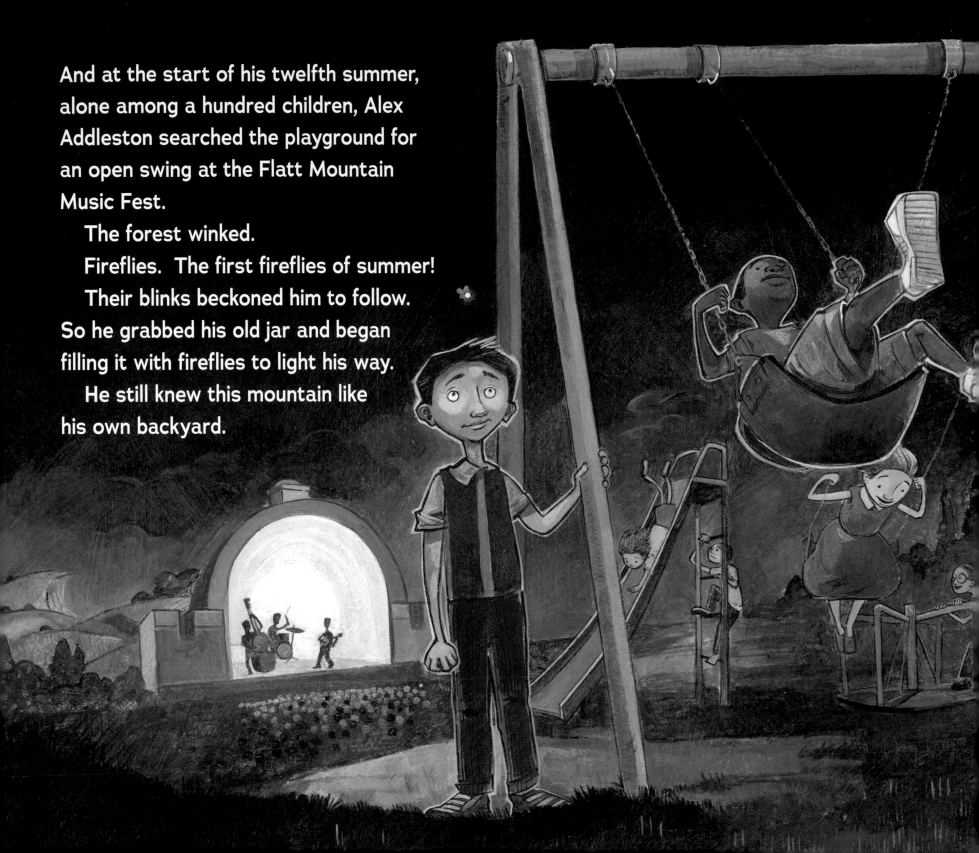

And at the start of his twelfth summer, alone among a hundred children, Alex Addleston searched the playground for an open swing at the Flatt Mountain Music Fest.

The forest winked.

Fireflies. The first fireflies of summer!

Their blinks beckoned him to follow. So he grabbed his old jar and began filling it with fireflies to light his way.

He still knew this mountain like his own backyard.

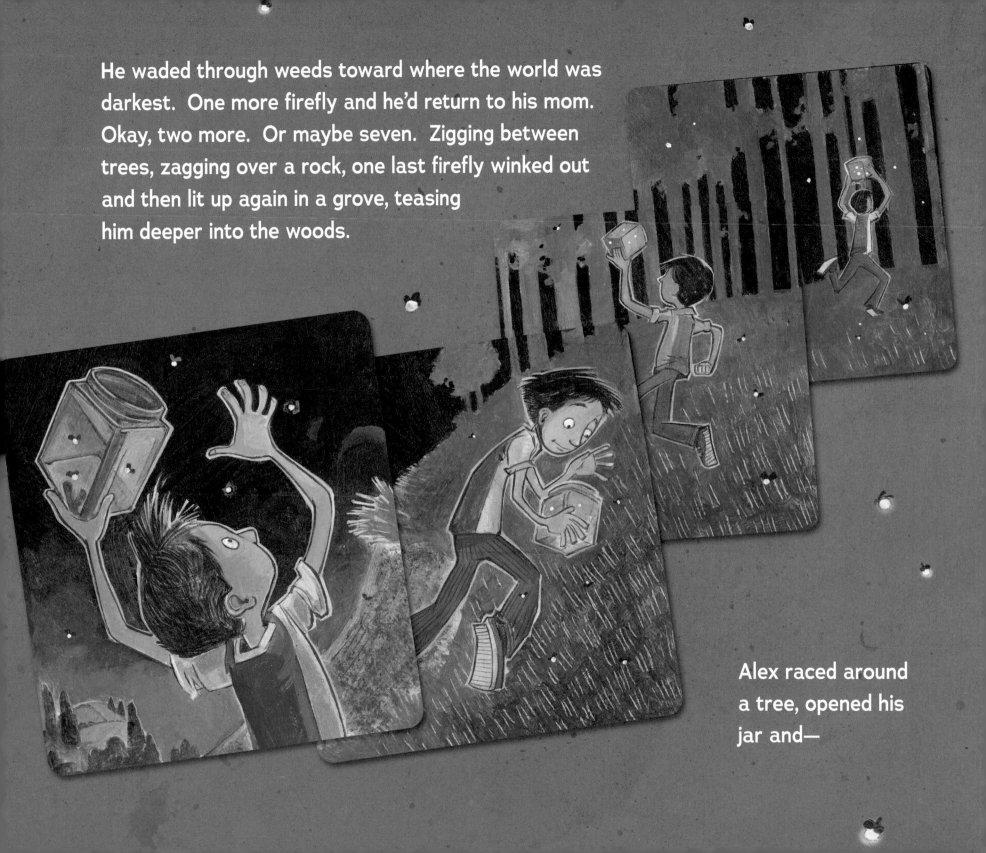

He waded through weeds toward where the world was darkest. One more firefly and he'd return to his mom. Okay, two more. Or maybe seven. Zigging between trees, zagging over a rock, one last firefly winked out and then lit up again in a grove, teasing him deeper into the woods.

Alex raced around a tree, opened his jar and—

Clank!

Jar met jar—the jar of a girl chasing the same firefly.

She looked like his best friend Alex. And yet she didn't look like Alex. But on her necklace, a Captain Moonbeam message ring glowed.

She seemed so tall and slim, so different from the kindergartner who had once squirmed into the same seat with him and started school on the same sheet of paper.

With six years of words piled up inside him, Alex didn't know what to say. He pulled his own message ring out of his pocket.

Slowly, Alex smiled. Then Alex did too.

"Harp slyamor?" they both asked.

"Me zippal fwip," came the double answer.